Chuckie's New Mommy

adapted by Kim Ostrow
based on a screenplay by Sarah Cunningham and Suzie Villandry
illustrated by Robert Roper

visit us at www.abdopublishing.com Reinforced library bound edition published in 2007 by Spotlight, a division of ABDO Publishing Group, Edina, Minnesota. Reprinted with permission of Simon Spotlight, Simon & Schuster Children's Publishing Division

SIMON SPOTLIGHT

An imprint of Simon & Schuster Children's Publishing Division 1230 Avenue of the Americas, New York, New York 10020 © 2002 Viacom International Inc. All rights reserved. NICKELODEON, *Rugrats*, and all related titles, logos, and characters are trademarks of Viacom International Inc. All rights reserved, including the right of reproduction in whole or in part in any form. SIMON SPOTLIGHT and colophon are registered trademarks of Simon & Schuster, Inc.

KLASKY CSUPO INC.

Based on the TV series *Rugrats*® created by Arlene Klasky, Gabor Csupo, and Paul Germain as seen on Nickelodeon®

Library of Congress Cataloging-in-Publication Data
This title was previously cataloged with the following information:
Ostrow, Kim
    Chuckie's new mommy / adapted by Kim Ostrow ; based on a screenplay by Sarah Cunningham and Suzie Villandry ; illustrated by Robert Roper.
      p. cm. -- (Rugrats ; 18)
    [1. Stepmothers--Juvenile fiction. 2. Babies--Fiction.] I. Roper, Robert, ill. II. Title. III. Series: Rugrats ; 18.
PZ7.O8545 Ch 2002
[E]--dc22
                                                           2002283017

ISBN-13: 978-1-59961-356-7 (reinforced library bound edition) ISBN-10: 1-59961-356-5 (reinforced library bound edition)

"Here I am!" shouted Chuckie as he burst through the bushes.

"Chuckie, you're opposed to wait until I finded you," said Tommy.

"Oh, yeah," said Chuckie. "I forgotted again."

Kimi popped out from behind another bush. "Here I am!" she cried happily.

"Uh . . . let's play something else," Chuckie mumbled.

As the babies headed for the sandbox Chuckie stopped short.

"Oh, no, here she comes," said Chuckie. "My new mommy's gonna do it again."

"Do what?" asked Tommy.

"She's gonna smoosh down my hairs," Chuckie said nervously. "I just know it."

"Hi, Kimi. Hi, Chuckie," Kira said. "Ready to go home?"

Chuckie tried to duck out of the way as Kira came closer, but it was too late.

"Is everything okay with Chuckie?" Didi asked Kira.

"I don't know," answered Kira. "I feel like we're not connecting. And with Chas working late these days, I worry that Chuckie may feel unsettled."

"Maybe Dr. Lipschitz can help," said Didi. "I'll call the 800 number and ask if they can recommend a book about new families."

Kira nodded. "That's exactly what I need."

Back at home Chuckie sat in his new big-boy chair and stared at the mountain of food in front of him.

"Kimi, what is this stuff?" he asked. "It looks like squiggly worms with mud balls on top."

"It's pasghetti and meatyballs!" said Kimi. "My mommy makes it all the time. It's her specialty."

"I never eated nuthin' like that afore," Chuckie grumbled.

Chuckie piled a meatball onto his fork and tried to eat it. But it wouldn't fit in his mouth.

"AH-CHOO!" Chuckie sneezed, and the meatball fell to the floor. "These meatyballs are so big, the sauce gets in my nose and gives me the sneezies," said Chuckie unhappily.

"They don't give me the sneezies," said Kimi. "And I eats them all the time."

Kira gently wiggled a tissue over Chuckie's nose. Chuckie squirmed in his seat.

"How am I opposed to blow my nose on a wigglin' tissue, Kimi?" asked Chuckie when Kira was gone.

"Mommy always holds my tissue," said Kimi. "I like it."

"Well, I don't," mumbled Chuckie. So he blew his nose the way he liked—on his sleeve.

After dinner Chuckie and Kimi got ready for bed. "I don't like these new jammies," Chuckie said. "My feets are trapped and I can't wiggle my toes."

"But they keep your toesies warm," said Kimi.

"My jammies gots feets, my meatyballs are sneezy, my hairs are smooshy," complained Chuckie. "Nothing's the same."

Just then Kira came in to say good night. "Sweet dreams," she said as she turned off the light.

"Looks like you needs a hug, Wawa," said Chuckie,
clutching his teddy bear. "At least we gots
each other. And that's never,
ever gonna change."

Later that night Didi dropped off a present for Kira. It was Dr. Lipschitz's bestselling book, *Step Up to Stepparenting.*

"'Chapter One,'" Kira read out loud, "'Connecting with Your Stepchild.'" She thumbed through the pages until she found a suggestion that sounded just right.

Kira headed upstairs to check on Chuckie and Kimi. As she smoothed Chuckie's hair Kira noticed his tattered teddy bear.

"Looks like somebody needs a makeover," she said to herself as she scooped up Wawa. "Chuckie will be so surprised!"

"Meatyballs . . . jammy feets . . . smooshy hairs . . . ,"
Chuckie moaned, tossing and turning in his bed. Then he felt
around for his Wawa. Chuckie's eyes popped open. "Wawa's
gone!"

At breakfast Chuckie slumped in his chair.

"What's wrong, Chuckie?" whispered Tommy.

"Nothin' is the same now that I gots a new mommy," Chuckie said sadly. "So Wawa runned away."

"When I gots Dilly, lotsa stuffs changed for me too," said Tommy. "But now everything's all better."

SPLAT! Dil threw a glob of cereal that landed on Tommy's head.

"I dunno, Tommy," said Chuckie. "Wawa's gone and he's never coming back."

"Sure he is, Chuckie!" assured Tommy. "We'll help you find him."

The babies toddled down the hall to look for the missing teddy bear.
"Maybe Wawa's in the lawn-tree room," Kimi suggested.
"He's not under here," said Tommy.
"Not in here, either," said Kimi.
Chuckie thought he felt something soft and warm in the sock basket.
"Wawa!" he shouted. But it was just Fifi taking a nap. Chuckie sighed.
"I'm never gonna see my Wawa again."

"There you are," said Kira. "I have a special surprise for you, Chuckie!" She opened the dryer and pulled out a freshly washed, newly dressed, cleaned-up teddy bear.

"Aaaaaaarggh!" Chuckie screamed. He knocked Wawa out of Kira's hands and ran upstairs.

"Chuckie! What's wrong?" cried Kira as she ran after him.

Chuckie's teddy bear had landed on Dil's bouncy seat. As Didi straightened the laundry room, Dil chewed on Wawa's ear.

Then he tore off the little vest that Kira had put on Wawa.

When Dil threw the bear up in the air . . .

. . . Wawa landed in a sudsy bucket, spilling it all over the floor.

Didi spun around. "Uh-oh, I think it's time to go!"

"I guess there's still a lot I don't know about you," Kira said sweetly, "like your favorite food, or your favorite games, or the stories you like." Kira moved closer. "It may take me a little while to figure it out, so until then, I'll tell you the one thing I do know. I know I have a new little boy who I love very much."

Chuckie looked up at his new mommy and smiled. But when she tried to smooth his hair, he cringed. And Kira finally understood. Instead of smoothing Chuckie's hair, this time she messed it up. Chuckie giggled and Kira giggled too. Then they gave each other a great big hug.

"Looks like Dil got a hold of Wawa," Kira said. "He's back the way you like him." She handed Chuckie the bear.

Chuckie hugged his tattered bear and smiled. "My new mommy may not be perfect, but she's mine!"